WITHDRAWN

P9-AFZ-352

ALFIE'S
LOST SHARKIE

For Rebecca Young

CLARION BOOKS
3 Park Avenue, New York, New York 10016

Copyright © 2014 by Anna Walker

First published by Scholastic Press, a division of
Scholastic Australia Pty Limited, in 2014.
First published in the United States in 2016.
This edition is published under license from
Scholastic Australia Pty Limited.

All rights reserved. For information about
permission to reproduce selections from this book,
write to trade.permissions@hmhco.com or to
Permissions, Houghton Mifflin Harcourt
Publishing Company, 3 Park Avenue, 19th Floor,
New York, New York 10016.

Clarion Books is an imprint of
Houghton Mifflin Harcourt Publishing Company.

www.hmhco.com

The illustrations in this book were executed in ink and collage.
The text was set in Chaparral and Marujo.

Library of Congress Cataloging-in-Publication Data is available.
ISBN 978-0-544-58656-7

Manufactured in Malaysia
TK 10 9 8 7 6 5 4 3 2 1
45XXXXXXXX

ALFIE'S
LOST SHARKIE

by ANNA WALKER

CLARION BOOKS
Houghton Mifflin Harcourt • Boston New York

It's time to get ready for bed, Alfie.

Where's Sharkie?

Who's Sharkie?

He has white fins,

sharp teeth,

scary eyes,

But I need Sharkie.

Let's see if he's in the bath.

He might be hiding in your pajama drawer.

He's not under here.

He's not in here, either.

Sharkie's gone.

Choose a book, Alfie.
It's time for a story.

Are you listening, Alfie?

Maybe Kitty took Sharkie!

I don't think Kitty took Sharkie. Let's finish the story and then see if Sharkie is brushing his teeth.

I'm not tired.

Pick a toy for bed, Alfie. We can look for Sharkie tomorrow.

Night-night, Alfie. Night-night, Sharkie.

Where's Bunny?

CONTRA COSTA COUNTY LIBRARY
31901059392508